Becka and the Big Bubble

All Around Town

**by Gretchen Schomer Wendel and
Adam Anthony Schomer**

Illustrated by Damon Renthrope

for Clayton and Megan

Published in 2009 by Windmill Books, LLC
303 Park Avenue South, Suite # 1280, New York, NY 10010-3657

Publisher Cataloging Data
Wendel, Gretchen Schomer
        All around town / by Gretchen Schomer Wendel and Adam Anthony Schomer ;
illustrated by Damon Renthrope.
                p. cm. – (Becka and the big bubble)
        Summary: Becka blows the biggest bubble ever, climbs aboard, and flies over the town.
        ISBN 978-1-60754-104-2 – ISBN 978-1-60754-105-9 (pbk.)
ISBN 978-1-60754-106-6 (6-pack)
        1. Bubbles—Juvenile fiction   2. Travel—Juvenile fiction
[1. Bubbles—Fiction   2. Travel—Fiction   3. Stories in rhyme]   I. Schomer, Adam Anthony
II. Renthrope, Damon   III. Title   IV. Series
        [E]—dc22

Printed in the United States of America

alphabet
soup

an imprint of

WINDMILL
BOOKS

New York

What do you think,
Blow some **bubbles** today?

Let's go outside.
Hooray, let's play!

The bubbles can get
As big as our heads.

"It's going to pop,"

My friend Ben once said.

It popped in my face

And in my hair.

Ben cheered me on—

Such a friend is quite rare.

"I'll do it again!"

I yelled without shame,

"Becka and The Big Bubble

That's my new name!"

I took a deep breath and closed my eyes.
I imagined a bubble on which I could fly.

A bunch of people gathered around.
I was standing on my own little mound.

Then Ben declared,
"Watch the most brilliant bubble blower in town!"

The crowd was so quiet—
No one made a **sound...**

This is the biggest bubble I had ever blown,
And can you believe it was here to be shown.

The crowd now gasped in pure delight,
Smile upon smile, Oh what a sight!

I climbed on top where I could sit.

My beautiful bubble, a perfect fit.

And like a dream I began to float.

Now this was a trip for all to take note.

I floated up past the store on my street.
The bubble could carry me faster than feet.

Mr. Jones from the bakery came running out the door.
"Wow Becks, what did you blow such a big bubble for?"

Then Jumpidi Jack
From across the way
Hopped so high
He made my day.

It was fun to float
With the bubble holding me up.
A dog howled in delight—
What a cute little pup.

And pretty Ms. Dawn of the chocolate store
Said seeing me fly inspired her s'more.

Even Pouty Pat, who's sometimes a frown,
Followed me smiling to the edge of town...

Where the wind grew fierce, way too high and then

I could not see town, Mom, Dad, nor Ben.

I felt kind of scared all alone way up here.

Then I thought, "There's nothing to fear!"

So higher I went, where there's so much to see—

How can I say it, **"Flippity-Free!"**

"I'll fly with my bubble to lands near and far

And see the whole world—I'll feel like a star!"

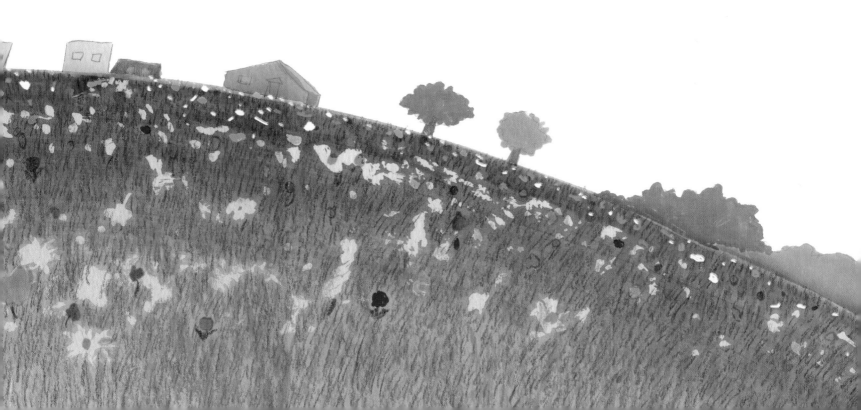

But in all the excitement, I popped my own bubble.
It now would appear that I was in trouble!

My bubble was now just magic in the air,

No longer a bubble, beyond all repair!

As I whizzed past the birds who were gliding with ease,

I thought of a plan that just might appease.

Two hands out wide, look at my feet,

Like a flying kite, **Swiftidi-Sweet!**

Like a kite I was gliding, much time now to blow—
Lickety-Split, another bubble to go!

"Thanks to the sky and the winds that we fly
And thanks to you double, my **second Big Bubble!**"

I floated on home to show Mom and Dad
All of the fun with my bubble I had!

Mom cheered me home, "A magic bubble, Woo-Hoo!"

"Yes!" I exclaimed, "Yippidi-Yoo!"

"Pop on in, time for supper I'm glad,"

Said my witty, wonderful Dad.

Pippity-Pop!

With the flick of my nail

To the ground I sailed...

What a day it had been!

Gretchen Schomer Wendel graduated from Michigan State University. After college she worked as a television reporter and writer on an award winning show in San Francisco. She has now written numerous children's books. Gretchen spends most of her spare time with her two children and her husband. They reside in San Diego, California.

Adam Schomer is a writer, actor, and improv comedian who was an All Ivy Athlete at Cornell University. Through soccer he explored the world, and it gives him great joy to share his traveling experience and life lessons through Becka. Adam continues to also write plays, sketch comedy, and animated TV.

Damon Renthrope is an award-winning illustrator in San Diego, California. After attending San Diego State University, he's created art for Rohan Marley, Mandy Moore, and various companies including DC Shoes, Sideout, Nascar, and MTV. He is most noted for his collection of caricature art, which features stylized portraits of famous faces. Selected works can be found on DamonArts.com.

You can go to www.windmillbks.com and select this book's title to find links to
learn more about Becka and her adventures, or to watch and listen to Becka online.